MISTLETOE AND MISFORTUNE

A TREEHOUSE HOTEL COZY MYSTERY (BOOK 4)

SUE HOLLOWELL

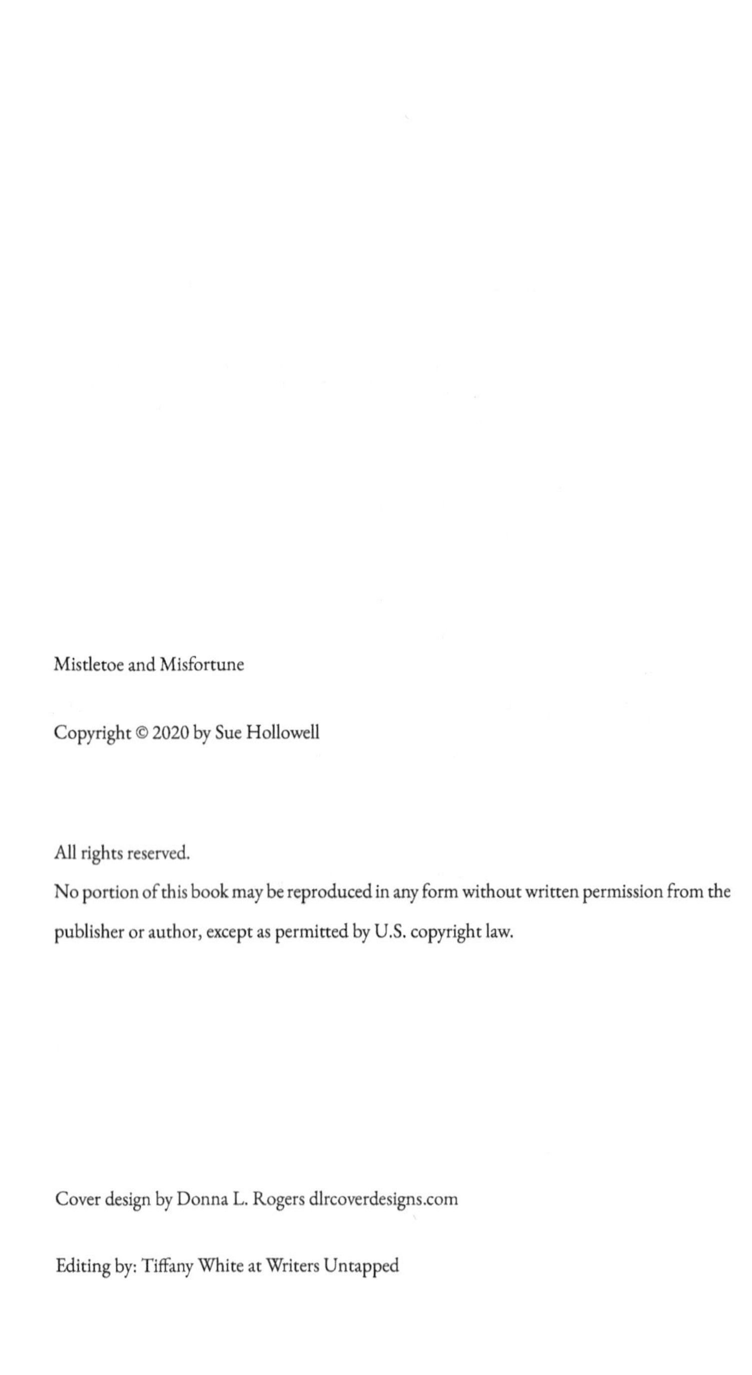

Mistletoe and Misfortune

Copyright © 2020 by Sue Hollowell

Cover design by Donna L. Rogers dlrcoverdesigns.com

Editing by: Tiffany White at Writers Untapped

Contents

CHAPTER ONE	1
CHAPTER TWO	8
CHAPTER THREE	14
CHAPTER FOUR	19
CHAPTER FIVE	26
CHAPTER SIX	32
CHAPTER SEVEN	38
CHAPTER EIGHT	45
CHAPTER NINE	51
CHAPTER TEN	57
CHAPTER ELEVEN	63
CHAPTER TWELVE	69
CHAPTER THIRTEEN	75

CHAPTER FOURTEEN 81

CHAPTER FIFTEEN 87

Hear From Max 92

Next Release - Crocuses and Corpses 93

Thank You 95

About the Author 96

CHAPTER ONE

Max trotted in front of me as we surveyed the location for the outdoor activities. Planning for the grand re-opening of the hotel had been underway for some time. A light dusting of snow had fallen the night before, giving an enchanting feel to the place. My heart warmed at how the expansion project had turned out. The two new units provided us additional capacity, and the lodge was a dream come true. My hopes for a town gathering place and a destination for out-of-towners was about to be realized. Max continued to high-step along the path that would host our sleigh ride on opening night. With the colder weather, I bundled him up in the cutest little red argyle sweater, and he wore it proudly. As we wove our way through the treehouses, I removed any branches that might be an obstacle for the sleigh. The layer of snow brought a peace to the day that I hoped would last.

"Chloe, two of my winter gnomes are missing." Mom's voice echoed as she came up the path from the other direction. She wore a coat that I was sure would have kept her warm at the north pole. She even wore appropriate footwear for the conditions, which wasn't always the case. "Max is always playing with them. What do you think he did this time?" she asked. She stomped toward us in her heavy boots. "I had them sitting around the firepit." She gestured behind her. "They looked so cute. And now they're gone."

Max and I caught up with her. "Are you sure they were there? You've got so many, I don't know how you keep track of them," I said.

Mom's gnome collection had somehow expanded beyond her backyard and infiltrated almost every place at the hotel. I initially agreed to allow a couple of them at the Cherry Cottage. Now we had an army of them.

She looked at me through the fur surrounding her large hood. "Believe me. I know where every single one of them are. They are my treasures." She turned and marched down the path ahead of us.

Max looked up at me and we both shrugged. We hadn't lost a gnome yet. I was sure they were here somewhere. It might just not be until spring that we'd find them. We trailed Mom as she led us to the location of the missing gnomes. I looked around. "Where's Trixie?" I called after her.

"She's sitting on the porch up at the office. I don't think she likes the cold very much," she said. Not a shocker that her princess dog wouldn't like the snow.

We approached the large opening, and I saw the workers had almost completed installing the lights. This would be a station where we served hot chocolate and gingersnaps on the night of the grand re-opening.

"See?" She pointed to a bench facing the firepit. Sure enough, a space on each side of the bench showed bare ground where something had previously been sitting.

Max took a step back. I looked at him. He took another step back. It wouldn't be the first time he was involved with shenanigans with those little creatures.

"I'll keep an eye out. For now, we need to keep focused on the setup for our event." I sat on the bench to catch my breath. Max jumped up beside me.

Mom walked around the entire firepit, looking everywhere for the missing gnomes. "Well, they didn't just walk off by themselves." She continued poking her head into the bushes.

I made eye contact with one of the workers installing the lights. He shook his head. "Mom, let's head back to the office. Harrison should be here any minute, and I want to warm up a bit."

She emerged from the shrubs with a huge grin. "Chloe, isn't it looking romantic here?" she asked, the gnomes now an afterthought. She had been not so subtly hinting about Paul and me going on a date. From day one of the hotel expansion, she was on a mission to make that happen.

"Remind me to come out here when it's a little darker to see how it looks when it's all lit up," I said.

Mom trailed behind me. "I'll ask Paul to do that with you." She giggled with her relentless pursuit of finding me a match.

We emerged from the trees just as I spotted Harrison's vehicle driving into the parking lot. My stomach tightened. I stopped. Mom sidled next to me.

"Harrison's here," she whispered. She looked up at me with tears in her eyes. "Oh, Chloe."

I yearned for reconciliation between the two of them. Harrison hadn't been in town since he was eighteen when he packed up everything he owned into a beater car and drove east. He and I had recent conversations to bring him up to speed with the hotel, Mom, and my sisters. I could tell he had softened toward Mom and the memory of our youth. But time would tell by how much when they actually spent time together in person. Mom took off like a shot, Max in tow.

Harrison, his wife Diane, their daughter, Julia, and her family exited the vehicle.

Trixie lumbered down the steps of the office toward the car and joined the welcoming committee. Mom stopped just short of the car and put her hand over her mouth. She and Harrison made eye contact. He held out his arms, and Mom moved forward into Harrison's embrace. The rest of the family came forward.

I joined them. Harrison gave me a hug with a long, firm squeeze. We released, and I grabbed his hand and stared into his eyes. "Harrison, I can't tell you what this means to me and Mom that you came."

He smiled. "I'm glad to be here. Let me introduce you to my family." He turned and gestured to his wife. I had never met any of them in person. Only one of the two daughters and family were able to make the trip. They were a lovely family. No matter what happened with the grand re-opening event, Harrison's visit was the highlight of the year.

I rubbed my arms to warm up. Max had instantly taken to the kids. Harrison's daughter Julia had a seven-year-old girl and a five-year-old boy. They were loving all over Max as Trixie ambled up to the trio. The pups would be in heaven with new playmates.

The adults gathered in a circle. "This place has really changed," Harrison said, gazing around. "It looks nothing like it did when I was here."

"Mom's done a great job keeping it going," I said. I looked at her. "And it's been quite a project with the expansion. I'm glad we're almost done with that."

Mom shook her head. She was eerily quiet, overwhelmed with emotion at Harrison's arrival. She'd never thought it would ever happen.

"We should show you around." Mom beamed proudly. "Let's go see our newest addition. I think the kids will really like the elevator to Crocus Castle." She waved the family on and headed down the path we had just come from.

I stood and watched the scene. My heart warmed my body from the inside out. I was still very surprised that Harrison had agreed to come, but I would take it. My phone in my pocket started to ring. I removed my mitten and reached in to retrieve it. I saw Paul's name on the caller ID. "Hi, Paul. What's up?"

Hearing Paul's name, Mom stopped and turned, her face plastered with a grin like Max's when he got gingersnap treats. She leaned over and whispered something to Harrison, which I'm certain had to do with Paul and me going on a date.

I looked away from her. And when Paul started talking, I grimaced.

Mom retraced her steps and returned to the parking lot. "Chloe?" she inquired.

I held up a hand to halt her questioning. "I'll be right there," I said into the phone. I hung up, my eyebrows furrowed. This couldn't be happening. I made sure the kids were occupied with the dogs before I said, "Paul needs me to come into the lodge right away."

"Chloe?" Mom repeated.

I took off toward the lodge and said over my shoulder, "I think you should stay here and visit. I'll let you know what's happening."

"Not on your life," I heard Mom say. "Harrison, why don't you guys get settled and I'll go with Chloe." She practically sprinted to catch up with me. The fireworks had already begun and our event was still days away.

CHAPTER TWO

An immense rush of warm air greeted me as I opened the hulking door to the lodge. Paul and his team had designed a beautiful, ornate twelve-foot-tall door made from pine to welcome our guests. The buzz from the number of people in the room was tenfold from what I would expect. I scanned the room to find Paul as Max sped past me. The fire roared in the massive rock-adorned fireplace, normally a cozy spot to gather and relax. Buffet tables had been set up to use for the sample food from the caterer. In the corner to my left a stage had been erected to host our entertainment for the event, a local, four-part harmony Sweet Adelines quartet, called the Cheeky Chicks. Mom and I stepped further into the room and closed the door.

Paul approached with his arms outstretched. "Chloe, I am so sorry." He looked at Mom and released a heavy sigh. "I don't know what happened."

Mom stepped around Paul and surveyed the room. "Who is that?" Mom yelled.

Paul turned and looked at the calamity. Right in the middle of the lodge, the head chef from the caterer was face down on the buffet table, surrounded by plates of meatballs, stuffed mushrooms, and strawberry goat cheese crostini. "It's Ben. It looks like he fell from the balcony. He's dead." Paul motioned to the upper level, which ran the entire perimeter of the lodge and was open to the first floor. The top plank of the railing was broken and had fallen onto the floor below. A small crowd huddled behind the broken rail, hugging the wall. "I have my crew getting some materials to patch that up for now and block it off." He looked at me, tears in his eyes. "This has never happened with one of my projects before. I'm so, so sorry."

I swallowed. The ramifications from this would be far-reaching. And I wondered if we would ever recover. "First things first, Paul. Thank you for having your crew take care of that."

At the end of the food table I spotted Haley's neon pink hair. Caroline's niece and apprentice at her candy shop had been offered the opportunity to provide the desserts for our event, her first official assignment. She sobbed into her hands.

"Mom, would you please go make sure Haley is OK?"

She dutifully fulfilled my request, and Max joined her. My boy, always the comforter.

I leaned in toward Paul and asked, "Are you OK?"

He rubbed his forehead and didn't say a word.

"Why don't we go up to the balcony and take a look? I can't imagine your work was faulty. There must be another explanation." I needed to enact some order in this chaos.

Silently, Paul and I ascended the grand staircase to the upper level. I stopped when we were at the top and turned to look over the scene below. Paul's crew had placed cones near the opening created by the broken rail and were in the process of shoring it up with a temporary piece of wood. We made our way to the commotion, where the volume of wailing grew louder.

Mom and Max had coaxed Haley away from the body to sit near the fireplace. Haley's pink head bobbed as she continued weeping. Max had a paw on Haley's back, consoling her. *That's my boy.*

"I think we should make a note of who is here and then get everyone out. We can tell them we need to regroup and we'll be in touch." I locked eyes with Paul. He was completely unfocused, understandably. "Paul."

His mouth opened with no response.

I touched his arm. "We'll figure it out."

Paul's crew began hammering and drowned out the cries of sorrow. He shook his head as if to clear the cobwebs. "I'll get everyone off the second level here." Paul moved over to the group congregated around the location where Ben fell.

Out of the corner of my eye I saw a buff-colored streak bolt from the fireplace up the stairs. Max approached with his mouth full of something. I didn't see him near the food table, but I wouldn't put it past him to sample some of the wares on his own. He trotted up to me, obviously proud of his prized possession. His head dropped and he released two candy truffles from his mouth in a slobbery mess.

"Where did you get that?" I asked him. I picked up the gooey mess to deposit it into the trash can.

Max turned around and faced downstairs. I wasn't quite cluing in to his message. Normally, he was pretty precise in his communication. His stubby little tail stuck straight out behind him as he tried to indicate his answer. I still wasn't getting it.

"Did you get this from Haley?" I asked.

He looked at me and barked. That noise completely silenced the entire room. Max tucked his head as if he was embarrassed at the outburst. He turned and returned to the staircase, going down five steps, and looked over his shoulder to see if I was coming. I followed as close as I could as he bolted to Haley's side.

Haley held a wad of tissues to her face, her eyes as pink as her hair. I didn't want to upset her further, but I had to ask. "Haley, are these your candies?" I held the slimy mess toward her.

She looked into my hand, then looked at me. "Oh, no. Was Ben eating that?" She paused and burst into tears.

Mom interjected, "What is that?"

I sat next to Haley, and Max jumped in between us, continuing to console her. "Max brought these to me. I think Ben may have been eating them when he died."

Haley's blubbering continued. I looked at Mom behind Haley's back. She mouthed *no*. I didn't want to believe it had anything to do with Ben's death either. But everything was on the table for now.

I stood. "Mom, would you please stay with Haley? I'm going to get some quiet outside and make a call to the Emerald Hills PD. I think they need to take a look at what happened." I contemplated the disaster. Things were going so well and on track for an amazing close to a fabulous year. What I saw before me changed all of that.

Poor Ben. And my heart broke for Paul. I could tell he felt responsible for Ben's death. I only hoped the investigation found otherwise. I opened the lodge door and felt the rush of cool air on my face—and the full-on reality of the situation. Not only might this delay our grand re-opening, it very well could taint the reputation of the hotel so badly we might never recover.

CHAPTER THREE

I took a deep breath and re-entered the lodge. I steeled myself for a very long day. I closed the door and leaned against it. Someone had covered Ben's body with a tablecloth. Paul had not made much progress in corralling everyone out. Understandably there was a lot of shock. Mom and Max continued to huddle with Haley near the fireplace. I'd leave them for now. I headed toward the staircase to evacuate the remaining crowd from the upper level. Paul's crew had completed the temporary fix to the railing and placed yellow caution tape and orange cones around the area. I slowly walked the length of the balcony, observing the top railing in the remaining area. It was possible that other areas might have that same issue as well. I looked around for Paul, and he was nowhere to be seen. I'd ask him to have his crew check the rest of it out to make sure it was stable. In the meantime, I had to scoot everyone down to the first floor.

A group of four women huddled relatively close to where Ben had gone through the railing. Janie, the lead of the Sweet Adelines quartet, scheduled to perform at our grand re-opening, was surrounded by the other members of the group. I slowly approached. "Ladies, I'm so sorry. I have to ask you to head downstairs so we can clear the place out."

The three members protectively moved in closer to Janie. They didn't budge. Janie's head lowered and the sobs began again. I moved down the balcony to another group whispering and pointing at Ben's body. I asked them to migrate downstairs and they complied. I continued along the balcony, shooing everyone from the area. I completed my round and returned to the Sweet Adelines. The woman closest to me turned, straightened up, and crossed her arms. Her eyes bore into me, daring me to disrupt them again.

I tried the honey-sweet approach before I had to bring out the vinegar. If they didn't comply with my request, the police would arrive soon enough to restore order to the scene. "Ladies, I know you must be very upset. You're welcome to stay. But would you please go downstairs for now?" I looked past the steely faced woman to elicit support for my request.

Nobody moved. I waited and stood my ground. They turned in toward Janie, continuing to console her. I remained there, the awkwardness escalating. Their whispers turned louder. One of them said, "Good riddance, Janie. You're better off without him." A loud bang from downstairs startled all of us. I peered in the direction of the sound and saw the buffet table where Ben had fallen had collapsed under his weight. As if this couldn't get any worse.

Janie picked her head up, eyes puffy and dripping, and wailed, "You just don't understand." She made eye contact with me and broke the circle. One of the women wrapped her arm around Janie's shoulder and began to escort her downstairs, shielding her from Ben's body. Janie's continued bawling echoed throughout the almost empty lodge.

I lagged behind the foursome to investigate what needed my attention on the main floor. I inhaled and slowly released my breath. Where to start? I was taken aback by Janie's reaction to Ben's death. And what was their relationship that she would be better off with him dead?

The quartet left the building. The crackling fire was the only noise that remained, the romance and warmth of the place long gone. I looked at the buffet table, splayed on the floor, plates and food scattered. I joined Mom and Max as they quietly sat by the fire. Max's head lay on Haley's shoulder.

Mom said without looking at me, "Chloe. This tragedy might ruin the hotel. After everything we did, it might all disappear." The words caught in her throat.

I reached over and took hold of her hand. "I know, Mom. But let's take one step at a time. We've both overcome tremendous obstacles in our lives. We can weather this too. I'm here with you. And we'll figure it out," I said with much more conviction than I felt. I needed Mom to be strong enough to keep me going as well. The hotel expansion took everything out of me. And I didn't know how much I had left to give.

"Chloe." I jumped, almost spilling Max onto the floor. I put my hand on my heart to slow down the patter. I turned to see Ty, the event photographer. I hadn't realized anyone was still inside with us.

"Ty, you startled me," I said. "What can I do for you?"

Ty always looked like he had just come from surfing the big wave. His shoulder-length curly blond beach hair draped his shoulders. I had never seen him with long pants. "I'm so sorry. I didn't mean to." Ty's chill personality helped to notch down my anxiety. He had been recommended by Caroline and was one of Haley's classmates. His youth disguised a very professional, experienced skillset as a photographer and videographer. I could tell it was his passion by reviewing his portfolio.

"I didn't realize anyone else was still here," I said.

He hoisted his camera bag over his shoulder. "I waited until you were free. I just wanted to see what you want me to do with the photos I've taken?" He held out his camera bag to emphasize his point.

I shook my head to clear some of the cobwebs. "Well, I guess you could send them to me. Of course I'll pay you for our agreed-upon contract."

"That's cool. Most of the pics I have are just me practicing the lighting. But it didn't seem right to continue after—" Ty pointed his elbow toward Ben.

I began escorting Ty from the building. "I agree. Send me what you have, and I'll let you know next steps." I opened the door for him to leave.

He turned to look at me. "This really sucks." He descended the steps and headed to his car.

"No doubt, Ty. No doubt," I mumbled.

Paul waved from across the parking lot. He jogged over and joined me as we re-entered the lodge. The expansive room, a place of joy and cheer just a short time ago, had turned somber and grim. He held my hand and maneuvered to re-join Mom and Max. We sat and waited in silence for the police to arrive.

CHAPTER FOUR

I hoped a new day would allow us to start with a fresh perspective. But truth be told, I didn't get a wink of sleep. From the looks of Mom, her disheveled hair, her robe still on, and her shuffling feet, it was the same for her. I had stopped at Caroline's to pick up coffee and pastries to jump-start our morning before heading to Mom's to figure out next steps. Buzz and the Emerald Hills PD had stayed late into the night at the hotel. My biggest hope was that Paul and his crew were not found negligent in the construction that led to Ben's fall from the balcony.

Max sped around the dining room table, obviously in no need of caffeine. As he passed Trixie's bed in the corner for each lap, he stopped and gave a sniff. She was having none of his early morning antics no matter how much he coaxed her.

I opened the lid of my travel coffee cup and sipped the hot liquid. I closed my eyes as it warmed my insides.

Mom joined me at the table. She stared at her hands in her lap. "This is so hard, Chloe. I'm just not sure I'm ready to talk about it."

I reached across the table and put my hand on Mom's arm. "I know." Max had settled in and was laying on my feet. His connection with me always gave me comfort. "But there are a lot of people counting on us. We have to move forward, at least for them."

Mom got up and pulled gobs of tissues from the box on the counter. She sniffed, dabbed her eyes and nose, and returned to her seat. "I just don't understand how this could happen?"

I pulled my notepad and pen from my bag. "I'll check in later with Buzz and get an update on what Emerald Hills has to say. Let's start by making a list of what we need to do."

Mom pulled a coffee cup toward her and wrapped her hands around it. "I need to check on my gnomes. I'm sure with all of those people traipsing around, they've gotten messed up somehow." OK, that response from her might just signal we're getting back to normal.

I wrote *check on gnomes* at the top of my list. "Great, what else?" I tapped the pen on my chin. "In general, let's do another walk-through of the grounds. I want to make sure the path for the sleigh is still clear. And that everything outside is still in good shape." I paused. I knew neither of us wanted to talk about the indoor activities, but we had to forge ahead. I started easy. "Ty had been doing some practice shots with the lighting. I'll take a look at what he sends me and get him some feedback."

Mom's phone rang and we both jumped a few inches in our chairs. She looked at me and frowned. "Who could that be?" She rushed to the counter to answer it, leaving her coffee sloshing onto the table.

I grabbed some napkins Caroline had tucked into our goodie bag and sopped up the mess. I couldn't figure out from Mom's side of the conversation who had called. She paced between the kitchen and dining room, with one-word answers to the caller. With Mom as the hub of gossip in this town, I was frankly surprised her phone hadn't been ringing off the hook starting at daylight.

She silently returned to the table after hanging up. She scooted the pile of coffee-soaked napkins to the side and grabbed her coffee cup again. She looked up and sighed deeply. "That was Marnee. She called to confirm that we still want them to cater the event."

Murano's Grill had been the go-to catering option for almost every event in town. With Ben, the owner, tragically dying, I was surprised his wife was so on top of the business side. But, like us, she had others to think about as well. "Did she sound like they would be able to do it?" I asked.

She shrugged and took a sip of her coffee.

Mom was holding something back. "Should we go see her in person? I'm concerned the shock hasn't hit her yet," I said.

Mom shook her head. "Chloe, it was odd. She seemed pretty chipper on the phone. Like she was happy to be taking charge of the restaurant."

"Well, shock hits people differently. I should probably stop by, at least to offer our condolences."

"You know, Chloe." Mom grabbed a stir stick and began swizzling her coffee. She looked up at me. "I didn't want to say anything before."

Mom was not usually one to keep her thoughts to herself. "What is it?" I asked.

"Well, the quality of Ben's food at the restaurant had really gone downhill recently. I was nervous about them catering for us," she said.

"Why didn't you say something?"

"There aren't many choices, and I hoped he could do it. But now we don't have to find out. Marnee said Carl, their sous chef, is trained and knows all of their recipes. She's confident he will do a great job. And he has always seemed like a nice guy too." She quit stirring and took several gulps of the coffee.

I returned to my list and added to it.

Catering: Carl will handle—stop by Murano's

"Maybe we should get a sampling of Carl's food, just so we know what we're in for."

"That's a good idea. When I tried Ben's meatballs at the sampling event, they didn't taste right. I couldn't place it, but they were just off. I thought maybe it was just me," Mom said.

"No, it wasn't just you. I thought the same thing. I'll definitely ask Marnee about that when I visit." I turned toward the door, hearing gravel crunching in the driveway. "Is someone here?"

Mom got up and smoothed her hair. It was either the caffeine or the prospect of seeing the guest that had put a spring in her step. "I'll get it." She unlocked the door and swung it wide open. "Good morning, Paul." She lightly bounced in her fuzzy slippers, avoiding my eye contact. Even in the midst of the tragedy, she had enchantment on her mind. "Come on in." She held the door for him, and I'm sure I heard the slightest giggle from her.

Paul carried a tray of coffee and a box of pastries from Caroline's. "I hope I'm not intruding." He placed the food on the table. "It looks like we've got enough for days."

Max rose from my feet and stood next to Paul, leaning into his leg. His tail furiously wagged, and he looked longingly up at Paul.

"OK, boy. I hear you. Priorities first." Paul crouched, gave Max a giant hug, and scratched him up and down his back. He looked over at

Trixie in her bed and held out his hand. She lifted her head in a greeting but moved no further. Paul crabbed-walked with Max in tow to give Trixie her greeting. "She's not spoiled, is she?" He chuckled and stood up.

Mom gestured to her chair next to me at the table and said, "Have a seat Paul. We're just going over a to-do list for the grand re-opening event." Mom scurried to the other side of the table, leaving the obvious opening next to me for Paul.

"Thank you, Mabel." He looked at Mom, then me. "I can't tell you again how sorry I am. I will do whatever it takes to make this right." He reached for a coffee, then placed his hand on the table.

"Paul," I said softly. "I don't think you had any fault in this. Your work is impeccable. There must be another explanation."

"Thank you for that, Chloe." He grabbed a coffee and placed it in front of him, blowing the steam. "What can I do to help?"

Mom jumped in, taking charge. "We're making a list of things that need to happen. We were just talking about Murano's still doing the catering. That's such a romantic place to eat. Don't you think, Chloe?"

I pursed my lips and gave Mom a wide-eyed look of *not now*.

Paul, completely up to speed with Mom's intentions, tried to help me out. "That is a nice place."

Mom grinned and sat back in her chair. Seed planted, fertilized, and watered.

"Paul, I hate to bring this up, but can you tell me the last things you remember Ben doing? That might help provide some clues to figure out this mystery?" I asked.

He took another sip of coffee and swallowed. "Of course. Mostly, he was downstairs at the buffet table, sampling the food along with everyone else. He had gone over to the dessert table and was trying some of Haley's candy. He was making faces, like he wasn't impressed."

I held my breath, not wanting to hear that. With Max's clue and now Paul's account, I just couldn't believe Haley would be at fault for any of this.

CHAPTER FIVE

Pearl had placed Max into the tub to suds him up for a bath. The warm water gently poured in the background, ready to rinse. Pearl chose one of Max's favorite shampoos, a huckleberry-scented treatment. She poured some into her hand and began scrubbing Max's ears. He closed his eyes and smiled. Pearl continued gently massaging the shampoo all over him. Max opened his eyes and tilted his head toward me, appreciation for this special experience in his gaze. Max was primping up for the hotel grand re-opening. I retained my optimism that we would get to the bottom of what happened to Ben and recover from the tragedy enough to celebrate our accomplishment. I needed to do this for Mom and all of the people that were counting on us.

Pearl continued kneading Max's muscles and weaving her fingers through his long fur. "Chloe, we haven't talked since Harrison arrived. How is that going?"

I sat in a chair several feet away from Pearl, next to her husband Buzz reading the newspaper. She worked her magic with Max. "Well, we haven't had a lot of time together yet. We got interrupted by Ben's fall. The initial greeting with Mom went well. That's the main thing I was wondering about. Harrison seems to be in a place of forgiveness."

Pearl grabbed the nozzle with a brush on the end and began rinsing. She methodically moved from head to tail, removing all of the bubbles. Max stood and shook to help along the water removal. Thankfully, I was far enough from him to avoid the spray. "I'm looking forward to catching up with him at the grand re-opening." She stopped and looked at me. "You are going ahead with it, aren't you?"

I looked at Buzz and back at Pearl. "I want to. I just don't know if we'll make it on our original schedule. There's still a lot up in the air."

Buzz grunted and turned a page in his newspaper.

I reached over and tapped the back of Buzz's paper. "Did you get an update from Emerald Hills PD?"

He lowered the paper onto his lap. "I don't know a lot yet, so I didn't want to say anything."

I scooted to the edge of my chair and tapped my foot. Max looked at me, his alert level raised. "Spill it, Buzz. What do you know?"

Buzz slowly folded his paper and set it on a side table. "OK. This is preliminary, so it's not to be shared."

I nodded. I would agree to any condition at this point in order to get the information out of him.

Buzz continued, "In addition to the fall, the toxicology report showed multiple poisons."

I gasped and my hand flew to my mouth. I shook my head. "It can't be."

Buzz stood and retrieved a towel you would find in a five-star hotel and handed it to Pearl. She wrapped Max, and he again closed his eyes as he was hugged tight in luxury. "I'm afraid so. There was more than one, so it'll take longer to distinguish what they were. Do you know more about this than you're telling us?"

Tears filled my eyes. "I don't know anything for sure. Only that Ben was seen eating Haley's candy just before he fell." Max leapt from the drying table and sped to my side. He placed a paw on my arm and laid his head on my lap. His still-moist fur left a wet spot on my pants. I petted him to affirm I would be OK.

"Chloe, that's serious. But let's wait for the final. There could very well be another explanation," Buzz replied.

I inhaled a deep breath to compose myself. "I know. This would devastate Haley."

Pearl approached Max with another towel and continued drying his fur. "I can't imagine what Marnee is going through."

"Yeah, she called Mom to confirm they could still cater if we wanted," I said.

Pearl finishing toweling off Max and tied a festive red bandanna with snowflakes around his neck. "I need to call her and see how she's doing. Her husband dying, having to take over running the restaurant. She's got to be a wreck."

I bent over and took in Max's smell. Scrumptious. He pranced around the room like he was performing for first place in a dog show. "You know, she didn't seem all that upset when she called. Maybe just putting on a brave face."

"Maybe," Buzz interjected.

Pearl and I both snapped our heads in his direction. Sometimes as the owner of Buzz's Barber Shop, he had more of a direct line to the gossip than we did.

Pearl pulled up a chair in front of Buzz and me. "Um, spill it," she ordered.

Buzz leaned back in his chair, crossing his legs and picking at an invisible spot on his shoe. I think he enjoyed being the one in the know.

"Well, I heard that Ben was possibly seeing someone on the side." He looked up, back and forth between Pearl and me.

"And I'm just now hearing about this?" Pearl asked.

Buzz stood up. "I have to go for my two o'clock appointment. I'll see you at home." He kissed Pearl on the top of her head. She waved her hand dismissively, forcing a smile. I'm pretty sure that wasn't the end of the conversation.

Pearl watched until the door closed after him. She looked back at me and grabbed a hold of my hands. "OK, now I want to hear the juicy stuff."

"Have you been talking to my mom?"

She released my hands. "No. But I'm sure it would be the same story. Are you going to go out with Paul?"

I moved over to the display case for all of the special pampering products Pearl had on the shelf. Max could use a couple more sweaters with the colder weather coming. I chose a blue and gray argyle and a green and white one with trees. "Can you add a couple of these to my bill?"

Pearl laughed. "Of course. But you're not getting off that easy. I see Paul's eyes when the two of you are together."

I joined her laughing. I would have to come to terms soon about whether I would go on a date with him. That's assuming he would even ask me out. "Well, let's just cross that bridge when we come to it." I tried everything to avoid the conversation.

Pearl placed the sweaters and another bottle of the huckleberry shampoo into a bag. "Would you say yes if he asked you?"

The heat rose from my neck to my face. I felt like I was in high school, wondering if I was going to get asked out by the hunky quarterback of the football team. I hadn't had that feeling in decades. It certainly livened up my life. "Now just isn't the right time. But someday. He is a wonderful person."

"I knew it!" Pearl blurted. "OK, keep me posted. I'll be thinking good thoughts for you two."

She handed me the bag and Max's leash. I left Pearl behind, giggling like a little girl.

CHAPTER SIX

T hankfully the snow had stopped and wasn't forecast to return until after the grand re-opening. I had to find out what happened to Ben. Max and I surveyed the hotel grounds again. This time with a very different purpose. I had my notebook and pen, ready to take notes for any clues we found. I figured we would cut a wide swath outside and slowly work our way in to where Ben landed. Max adorned one of his new sweaters, and we strolled the path that wove through the trees to each treehouse. We carefully surveyed each unit, stopping to look around. The snow muffled most every sound. The only noise emanated from critters searching for food. I hoped that wasn't too much of a distraction for Max. I was pretty confident when he was on a case; he was laser focused on his job.

We visited Crocus Castle and Cherry Cottage. We completed our rounds to the rest of the units and headed to the open firepit. This was such a beautiful gathering place and had potential for so many wonderful memories. Nothing stood out as suspicious so far. I plopped down on the bench and Max leapt up beside me, leaning his head on my shoulder. I returned the gesture.

"Max, I just don't know what to think at this point." I made a note of what we had checked and got up to finish canvassing the hotel grounds. We traversed the route the sleigh would travel and removed twigs newly fallen onto the path. Still nothing. "Let's head inside, Max."

We emerged into the parking lot and headed to Lily Lodge. A beautiful, elegant name. I chose to believe it wouldn't be tainted forever. "Max, we only have four more days to solve this." He barked and jumped up and down, more confident than I felt.

The cleaning crew had arrived early to prepare for a re-do of the event preparations. Max and I stepped inside to continue inspecting. We paused on the other side of the door to examine the interior of the lodge. The grand fireplace lay dormant, giving an ominous feel to the place. Workers continued their chores as Max and I climbed the staircase. I imagined myself as Ben, making his final walk to the railing. The temporary structure was still in place. I stepped to the back wall where Janie and the quartet had gathered after Ben had gone over, scanning the expanse of the lodge. What was I missing? The railing had obviously given way to Ben's body. But if the fall hadn't caused his death, what else was going on?

I needed to get another angle. Why wasn't I seeing it? Max and I moved downstairs to my favorite feature in the lodge. We sat on the hearth. I made a couple of other notes of what we had looked at. Sometimes ruling things out made the suspicious more obvious. I hoped we would get there in this case.

"Max, I need to let Caroline know about Haley's candy. I believe in my deepest being that it had nothing to do with Ben's death. But if this gets out, Caroline needs a heads-up."

Max rose and looked at me. He leapt from the hearth and began prancing the perimeter of the lower level, stooping frequently to sniff. The spot where he had been sitting was a puddle of melted snow. He must have tracked that in on the bottom of his furry paws. Could the floor have been slippery where Ben was? I made that note. *Great job, Max!*

I dialed Caroline's number and held my breath, secretly hoping she didn't answer and I could defer this difficult conversation. No such luck. "Hi, Chloe." She was chipper.

I closed my eyes and swallowed. "I just wanted to give you a quick update from Buzz," I said.

"Oh no, Chloe, what is it? Was it the railing?" she asked.

I inhaled, and as I slowly let my breath out, I said, "Not exactly." I paused, forcing the words. "The toxicology report showed some poison."

I didn't get anything else out before she gasped, loud enough that Max turned and looked at me with concern. I nodded and he returned to my side.

"I'm so sorry, Caroline. I wanted to let you know in case word gets out," I said in a shaky voice. So many lives impacted by this catastrophe.

Caroline sniffled. "Thank you. I won't say anything until we know for sure."

We hung up and I pulled Max in close to me. He had something in his mouth I hadn't seen until now. He turned and deposited it onto my lap. It was a pitch pipe used by the quartet. It befuddled me how he uncovered these clues. I hugged him tight and looked down at my phone. I would have given anything not to have made that call to Caroline. Haley was an up-and-coming chef with remarkable talent. I couldn't let my mind go any farther with the possibilities. The green notification light blinked, reminding me that I had an e-mail from Ty with the photos from the other day. I didn't want to go there either, but we had to forge ahead.

Max and I moved from the fireplace hearth to an oversized love seat. We sunk into the luxurious cushions, and I downloaded the pictures from Ty. I set my notebook and pen to the side, ready to capture any additional clues.

Ty's pictures were incredibly good. Seeing the talent and skills of these young people warmed my heart. I could tell both Haley and Ty were following their passions. Even though these pictures were a trial for the lighting, they were good enough to be the final version, in my opinion. I always marveled at how many were taken. I must have had over a hundred. As I scanned through, it looked like this was just a partial set of the interior activity. There were several photos of Haley to start this off. Did Ty have a crush on her? The photos continued throughout the lower level, capturing the buffet table and the stage where the Sweet Adelines would perform. He had closeups of plates of food that looked real enough to eat. Max looked at me as drool seeped from his mouth. My boy always made me smile.

The second half of the pictures captured the upper level from the fireplace vantage point. The before pictures stunned in capturing the authenticity. I swiped through the slideshow to stop right at the point Ty had recorded Ben's fall. Ben's body was up against the railing facing the floor below and Janie's arms were outstretched, reaching toward Ben, her mouth open in a silent scream. I continued swiping like I was watching a slow-motion movie. Ty's camera must have been on automatic to capture each movement as Ben plunged to his death. After his fall, Janie had retreated to the wall with her quartet, her hands over her face.

Max whimpered and looked at me. I set my phone down. Did Janie have something to do with Ben's fall? Why would the two of them be together upstairs when Ben should have been overseeing the setup of the food samples? Did she know more about what happened than she let on?

CHAPTER SEVEN

I settled onto the living room couch at Mom's for a visit with Harrison and family. This would be the first real interactions I would see between them. Not gonna lie, my nerves were on high alert. Max jumped up next to me, followed by Harrison's two grandkids. Max moved in between them for the most attention. He soaked up every second of the extra pampering. The others took a seat for our visit.

"This is great coffee from Caroline's," Harrison said. "And her pastries look to die for."

I nibbled an apple fritter. "There was a time her business wasn't doing well at all. I'm glad it's come around. She spoils Max with his favorite gingersnap treats every time we're in there. Kids, there's some in the box if you want to go get them." Christina and Russell scrambled to the kitchen to be the first to grab the treats. Max flew behind them. He turned and looked at me when he got to the kitchen. I nodded.

"Mom, where's Trixie?" I asked.

Mom hoisted herself from her chair and peeked into the dining room. She pointed. "She's right there in her bed."

I bent over to spy on her through the dining room table legs. "Hmmm. Is she OK?"

Mom returned to her chair and plunked down. "Of course she's OK. Why wouldn't she be?"

I needed to choose my words carefully. I didn't want a scene with Harrison's visit just beginning. "She seems so lethargic lately. I'm just worried she's gaining too much weight for that little body."

Mom waved my comment away. "Harrison, she's such a worrier, isn't she?"

Harrison smiled warmly and looked at us both. His eyes twinkled. He was actually enjoying this. Small talk continued, everyone dancing around the elephant in the room. Finally, Harrison quietly asked, "Chloe, is there anything I can do to help with the lodge?"

I shook my head. "Thank you. Not right now. We're still waiting to hear from the police on the final report." I had to keep the news of poisons to myself for now.

He got up and refilled his coffee in the kitchen. "OK. I don't know what your plans are for the caterer, but if you need me to cook something up, I can." He returned to his seat.

I was so proud of my little brother. He seemed to truly have forgiven Mom and was treating her well. And back home he ran a successful gourmet restaurant. "I appreciate that. But you're here visiting."

"OK. But seriously. Let me know if you need me. I'm happy to do it," Harrison said.

Mom stood and stepped to the center of the room as if to deliver a speech. She leaned over with wide eyes that locked into mine. "Chloe, that would be a dream come true. Harrison coming back to open a restaurant here." She returned to her seat, crossed her legs, and grabbed her coffee, satisfied she had set her plan in motion.

With dead silence in the room, all I could hear was Max crunching gingersnap treats. Where in the world did the conversation go from here?

I cleared my throat. "I'm meeting with Marnee to talk about the catering. When she called Mom the other day, she seemed confident they could still provide the food. But if that changes, I'll let you know."

Mom scooted to the edge of her chair. "I'm actually skeptical she can do it. Her husband died. He's the chef. He runs the restaurant."

Harrison looked at her. "Sometimes in a tragedy, people step up when they have to. Then when reality hits later, they break down and grieve."

I interjected. "From what I understand, she's trained as a chef too."

Mom snapped her head my direction. "Well then, why wasn't she doing the cooking?"

I shrugged and set my cup on a side table. "Who knows? I'm just glad they're able to do it. I have bigger things to worry about. Like explaining Ben's death so we can continue with the event. Time is ticking and there aren't many answers."

Mom rose and placed a coaster on the side table. She pointed at my cup and the coaster. I complied. She plopped down in her chair. "I heard Janie and Ben had a thing."

My mouth opened. Was I the last one to know these things? I made a mental note to check in first with Mom from now on if I needed to know the town happenings. "I did hear that rumor."

She looked at me. "From who?"

"Buzz," I said. "When Max was getting his trim at Pearl's the other day. I was surprised he was in the know for something like that."

Mom laughed. "Men are sometimes more gossipy than women. And with that barbershop of his, he's in a prime spot to hear the goings-on. I even stop by there to keep up with Buzz on what's happening."

That was quite a sight to ponder. My mom and Buzz exchanging grapevine topics.

"Anyway," Mom continued. "I guess he ended the relationship. Janie wasn't happy about that. He'd apparently promised to leave Marnee and marry her. She already had plans for a house bigger than he had with Marnee and for lots of kids."

I picked up my empty coffee cup and napkin and headed toward the kitchen. I placed my cup in the sink and napkin in the garbage. The kids still sat on the floor with Max, nibbling treats. My heart warmed at the apparent mutual joy between them.

I returned to the living room and stood in the doorway. "Mom, how do you know so much about Janie?"

She gathered empty cups and napkins and marched toward the kitchen with a slight shake of her head. "Chloe, I'm a cultured person, if you didn't notice. I support the arts."

I looked at Harrison and lifted my hands, not sure what that was about. "OK, Mom."

She returned to the room and looked down her nose at me. "Every year I attend the barbershop performance. Janie's quartet always performs. After the show in the lobby, I see her and Ben together, like co-conspirators. It's been obvious for a while that something was going on between them." She returned to her chair, smoothing an invisible wrinkle on her robe.

It took everything I had not to bust a gut laughing. I didn't know why I found that funny. But sometimes Mom came from left field, which kept me on my toes. My phone began ringing. Pulling it from my purse, I saw Paul calling. I held up a finger to the room and answered the call, moving to the bedroom for some privacy. Max's gaze followed me; he was always on alert with my movements. Thankfully, it wasn't bad news. Paul was just checking in to see if there was anything he could do to help.

I returned to the living room, my face feeling like it was on fire. I averted my eyes from everyone.

"That was Paul, wasn't it?" Mom giggled. Dang, even after all these years. What kind of special powers did Mom have? "Paul likes Chloe. And it's only a matter of time before they go on a date," Mom said to the room at large.

She looked at me. I continued avoiding eye contact. I peeked up at Harrison, who grinned from ear-to-ear. Oh, geez. Now he was in on it too.

"OK, yes it was. He was just checking in. You do realize we have a business relationship, right?" I sat down and returned my phone to my purse, crossing my legs in defiance. Max returned to the room and stood in front of me, locking eyes. I reached to pet him. "All right. I'm considering a date with him—if he asks."

Mom clapped. Max jumped into my lap and began licking my face. Laughter erupted in the room. I nudged Max to the side and stood. "I think this would be a good time for me to go. Plus, I'm going to Murano's to confirm catering plans. Marnee assured me that Carl can step into Ben's shoes, and I'm going to grill him to make sure."

Max and I attempted a graceful exit. If the prospects of my date with Paul could be a topic that united my family, I'd gladly make the sacrifice.

CHAPTER EIGHT

Max and I circled the block three times before we located an open parking spot. We rounded the corner to the front door of the Murano Grill to be met by a line of waiting people. Maybe the restaurant was getting sympathy business with Ben's passing. We edged our way along the sidewalk to the front.

I felt the need to inform people we weren't cutting the line. "I've got a meeting with the owner about catering," I said to the group in general. A few initial glares turned into nodding heads.

Max and I squeezed through a mob in the lobby and reached the hostess stand. The teenage-looking girl frowned at me. The tendrils of hair in her bun had escaped the clasp. "You'll have to wait in line," she said, indicating the hoard of bodies.

I smiled, sure that she was completely overwhelmed at the moment. "I've got an appointment with the owner to plan the catering for an event."

The hostess hugged menus to her body. Tears formed in her eyes. The tragedy of Ben's death right at the surface. "I'll let Marnee know you're here." She turned and was swallowed by the crowd.

I stepped to the side, away from the traffic of customers coming and going. The wall opposite my location had several rectangle spots open where it appeared picture frames once were displayed. The odd assortment remaining in a haphazard pattern were a combination of Marnee posing with customers and awards won by the restaurant.

The hostess emerged into the opening and said, "Marnee will be right here." She returned to the stand and studied the table layout, then called a group of customers to be seated.

It wasn't long before Marnee appeared from the same direction the hostess had come, her bright pink sparkling cat-eye glasses almost lighting her way. She smiled wide and reached out to shake hands. "Hi, Chloe." She waved her arm around. "Isn't this wonderful? We haven't been this busy in ages." She turned and over her shoulder said, "Follow me. We'll go to the office where it's quieter." She led me through the gauntlet to a little sanctuary just off the kitchen. "Whew. I'm glad for a break. We've been going nonstop." She sat behind the desk.

I slowly lowered myself into the guest chair. I was stunned and had to force words out. How could she be acting as if her husband hadn't just died? She seemed to be on top of the world. "Thank you for taking the time." I looked over my shoulder at the beehive of activity in the kitchen. "I'm so sorry about Ben." I hadn't seen Marnee since he had died. "I'm sure we'll get to the bottom of it."

"Thank you. Now, I'm sure we can still handle your catering. I've promoted Carl to head chef, and he has stepped right in. We haven't missed a beat." Marnee pulled out a recipe book and placed it on the corner of the desk. She opened the notebook and flipped through the laminated pages to the hors d'oeuvres sections. "So here's what we're thinking. Keep the stuffed mushrooms and strawberry goat cheese crostini and swap the meatballs for chicken sates." Marnee looked up as the doorway darkened. "Oh, good timing."

I turned in my chair to see Carl, the new head chef at Murano's. More accurately, I smelled him before I saw him. The overwhelming odor of cigarette smoke rolled past me. I held my breath and returned to face Marnee.

Carl stepped into the room to join the conversation. His chef's jacket was unbuttoned and hung sloppily on his shoulders. His pants appeared to be multiple sizes too large and ready to drop to his ankles.

I looked at him, not as confident as Marnee that he could pull this off. "I thought the meatballs were a specialty. I was looking forward to them."

Carl stepped up to the notebook and flipped a few pages. "They were Ben's specialty. But honestly, we all just tolerated them." He held his hand to the side of his mouth, whispering in a conspiratorial way, "They weren't that good."

Marnee laughed. She tipped her chin and peered at me over her shimmering glasses. "They actually made me sick. So Chloe, what do you think? Is everything a go?"

By all appearances, they had their act together. But something in my stomach was rumbling. It wasn't from hunger or that hideous smell from Carl. I scooted to the edge of my chair and slowly turned through the notebook pages. I looked up at Carl. "Do you have a specialty?"

Carl stepped back and leaned against the wall, crossing his arms. "I can handle anything. What do you want?" He glanced at Marnee and smirked.

"I was just asking. This is fine," I said.

Marnee reached toward me. "Trust me. This will be our best catering job yet." Her eyes sparkled as much as her glasses. She looked at Carl and back at me. "I have big plans for this place. Now that I'm in charge I can finally live my dream and run this place the way it should have been all along." Marnee stood and went to the door. I took that as a sign our meeting was adjourned.

I followed her. "Thank you, Carl. I look forward to tasting your work."

"Yeah," he said and returned to the kitchen.

Before I was out of earshot, I heard Carl yelling at his staff. For Marnee's sake, I hoped she had made the right decision to promote Carl and accept his changes. Murano's did well before this misfortune. So far it appeared it was doing even better after.

Marnee stopped at the hostess stand and hugged me. I smiled, said, "Thank you," and fought my way through a crowd that had almost doubled in size since I entered. What did I know about the restaurant business? I probably would have fired Carl because of his attitude. But whatever they were doing appeared to be highly successful.

I got in my car and closed the door, returning to peace and tranquility. Max immediately turned his head and put his paw over his nose.

"I know, buddy. It's Carl. He was smoking like a chimney and smelled very greasy." Max laid down and put his second front paw over his eyes and whimpered. I started the car and opened both windows to air us out on the way home. I'd have to toss my clothes in the laundry. I didn't begrudge Marnee one second of her success. But so soon after

Ben had died, and all traces of him at the restaurant had disappeared. It was almost as if she had been just waiting for him to be gone so she could take over.

CHAPTER NINE

Max and I really needed some alone time. Before we settled in for the night at Buttercup Bungalow, we made one more trip around the hotel. Most everything was quiet, allowing the fog from my brain to dissipate just a bit. I pulled out my notebook to jot down any clues we might discover. The snow from the other day still blanketed the grounds, making it look picture perfect. I would have to ask Ty to get some of those shots for marketing material. With the combination of the beauty and a romantic setting, I hoped our reservation book would fill up and draw steady crowds. Our new lodge would be the perfect place for small retreats or even larger conventions.

Max and I continued our rounds. The exterior of the hotel was in great shape for our event. All we needed were the people to bring the joy.

We entered the lodge, an ominous feeling to the expansive building. Why couldn't we figure out what had happened to Ben? Maybe the stress of it all was cramping our brains or we were trying too hard. Some relaxation was in order to regenerate some brain cells. I slowly traversed the first floor, covering every inch. Nothing. I continued my trek up the stairs. I stopped on the landing and turned around, looking high and low, hoping an inkling of a clue would appear. Nothing. I would make one trip around the balcony and then call it a night. We walked by the repaired railing, my stomach now in my throat as I relived that treacherous fall. This couldn't be the end for the hotel. It just couldn't.

Max sped ahead of me to a bench along the wall. I followed him, looking for anything out of place. This was getting us nowhere. "Max, let's just call it a night and start fresh tomorrow." He turned and looked at me with something in his mouth. I crouched and retrieved a pair of neon green sparkly glasses from him. These were identical to the pair Marnee had been wearing, except a different color. What were they doing here? I examined the floor around the bench to see if there was anything else. I'd give her a call in the morning to confirm we had found her glasses. She must've been missing them.

We headed downstairs and off to our sanctuary. My head was about to explode with everything going on: worry about Harrison's visit and how he and Mom would get along; stress over the grand re-opening; and if all of that weren't enough, a dead chef right in the middle of the preparations. From my visit with Marnee, it appeared there was no love lost between the two of them.

Max and I settled into one of our favorite spots in the Buttercup Bungalow. One of these days, we might have to move into our own house so we could rent this place to guests, but it had really grown on us.

I got our puzzle book, Max's gingersnap treats, and a huckleberry cocktail for me. This was just what the doctor ordered. I chose a medium difficulty classic sudoku puzzle for us. I looked at Max, and he rested his snout in the crook of my elbow. His eyes drooped. Maybe we weren't up for a puzzle tonight. I sipped my drink, pondering what we knew about Ben's death. My phone vibrated with an e-mail notification from Ty. He had sent another batch of photos from the other day.

I was torn whether to look at them tonight. Max lifted his head, now fully awake. *OK, pictures it is.* I leaned over so he could see the screen. More stunning photos that almost made the place look better than it actually was. I wondered what type of filter he used to get that effect. So many choices for the brochures.

I swiped through, looking at the pictures with awe. The work Paul had done made our dream come to life with the expansion of the hotel. We really owed him for that. I couldn't stop looking. There must have been over a hundred shots in this second batch.

Max stood, his body stiffening and his tail pointing straight back.

I looked at him. "What is it, boy?"

I petted him. He didn't budge. We had both been through a lot the last several days. Maybe a gingersnap would soothe him. I reached for a cookie and held it out. He turned his nose away. I was not getting the message. I really did need a good night's sleep. Unable to figure it out, I returned to my phone. I swiped to the next picture and saw it. How in the world did Max know?

Ben and Janie embraced in front of a door at the Emerald Hills hotel. This picture was obviously not meant for me. The quality was grainy and it was taken from across a parking lot. I hesitated with my next move. Should I call Ty and let him know what he had sent me? Why would he be taking pictures of them? This appeared to confirm what Buzz and Mom said about Ben having an affair.

Max tapped his paw on the phone. I looked at him. We had gone this far, might as well continue. More photos of Ben and Janie followed. Laughter, love in their eyes, holding hands. It just went on. "Max, I at least need to call Buzz about this." He barked, excited that we had progress on the mystery. I was glad he felt confident. I was more confused than ever.

My phone vibrated with an incoming call, startling me so much I almost pitched it across the room. My heart raced as I saw Paul's name on the caller ID. I would soon have to acknowledge the giddiness I felt about him. Setting aside all of the crazy times, deep down I did really want him to ask me out. It was time for love in my life again, and I wanted it to be him.

I took a deep breath before I answered, then smiled. "Hi Paul."

Max grinned from ear to ear. He jumped down from the love seat and barked, unable to contain his excitement about Paul.

Paul chuckled. "I hope it's not too late, Chloe."

"Not at all. What's up?"

Max continued his happy dance all around the treehouse.

"I just wanted to let you know I'm going to have my crew look at all of work tomorrow to make sure everything is safe. I don't want you to worry that something like this will ever happen again." His voice cracked. He was understandably torn up about this.

"That's wonderful, Paul. Thank you and your crew for the care." Max returned to his spot next to me, his chin on my thigh. "Honestly, one thing I'm confident of is that the railing wasn't faulty. I know there's another explanation; I just don't have that yet."

"Chloe, that's very kind of you to say. Let me know what else I can do. I want this event to be spectacular for you and your mom. I know what it means and how hard you've worked."

"Thank you." We said our goodbyes. I looked down to see Max's eyes closed. I agreed. *Let's call it a night.*

CHAPTER TEN

I immensely enjoyed Harrison and his family's return to Cedarbrook. I hadn't realized how much I missed him. Today's visit at Mom's would tell the tale. The entire Carson clan would be in attendance. I expected a circus atmosphere, but in a good way. After all this time, Mom was getting her wish of her kids reunited, at least for a short period of time. Truthfully, I couldn't have been more skeptical that it would happen. But she always believed.

Mom's driveway and the cul-de-sac was full of cars. I parked at the end of the line. Max and I wove our way to the front door, hearing voices as far away as the end of the sidewalk. Max pranced alongside me, anxious to reach the crowd and all of those hands to pet him. I pulled open the door and he shot through and disappeared beyond the scores of legs. My sister Zoe was nearest the door and stood to greet me. She put her arm around my shoulders and guided me in. All heads turned my way, and I was heralded with shouts of "Chloe!"

I joined the frivolity. The energy in the room was palpable. I found Mom and hugged her tight. She pulled me away and looked into my eyes. "Chloe, I'm so happy." She glowed. We sat down, Mom seated at the head of the circle. "Harrison was just telling us more about his restaurant." Mom signaled Harrison to continue.

Harrison got up and snagged another pastry. "Why don't we let someone else share for a while? I'm probably boring you with all of this restaurant talk."

Mom waved her arm back and forth. "No, no. Keep going. I have an idea that's percolating." She beamed. There was no telling what was brewing in her head. I had an inkling, but only because I had been spending so much time with her these recent months for the hotel expansion. I was pretty sure none of my siblings would go for it, though. I hoped their decline of her offer didn't break her heart.

Harrison swallowed his bite and shrugged. "OK, but I want to catch up with Zoe and Joey too." He continued, "My philosophy with the restaurant is to use as many locally sourced and sustainably harvested ingredients as possible. The freshness creates an unparalleled taste. One of the customer favorites is my Humboldt Fog goat cheese salad."

Mom's eyes practically sparkled. She scooted to the edge of her chair. "That sounds heavenly," she said and licked her lips. She looked around, taking stock of this beautiful family moment. My heart warmed.

Harrison laughed. "It is. It's got fresh goat cheese, seasonal fruit, and candied hazelnuts."

"So Harrison," Mom started, forming her hands into a steeple in front of her.

Harrison panned the room, bracing for the reveal of Mom's brainstorm. "Yes?"

My sisters and I watched Mom and Harrison like a tennis match.

"I have an idea. Don't say no. Just say you'll think about it," Mom said. She waited for his response.

Joey looked at me and mouthed "What?". I held up a finger signaling her to wait just a second. I didn't actually think it was a complete harebrained idea. It had potential. But it required the whole family in order to succeed.

Harrison looked to me for guidance. "Chloe?" Everyone looked my direction.

This was all Mom's doing. I gave her the floor to speak. As if on cue, she stood to give one of the most persuasive talks of her life. She stepped forward and cleared her throat, straightened up, and jutted her chin forward. "I think we should open a family restaurant together." She stopped to let that land. Slowly she looked at each of her four kids to assess our reaction. It was dead silent.

My heart cracked. I didn't want her feelings hurt, but that was a monumental ask of four adult families. I hoped my vibe in the room permeated their response to at least let her down easy.

I couldn't stand the silence and took the lead. "Mom, that's an interesting idea," I began, looking around for the next response.

Every single one of them averted their glance. I widened my eyes, compelling someone else to speak. I tilted my head slightly toward Zoe. She was likely the next most diplomatic person.

Zoe stood. Somehow this seemed to be evolving into a formal speaking event. "Well, we could certainly contribute quite a bit from our farm." Zoe and her long-time boyfriend had developed an off-grid lifestyle. With their animals and produce, they fed themselves, sold at the local farmers market, and bartered for what they needed. I was stunned at her encouraging response.

Mom plopped in her chair, started clapping, and bounced in her seat. "That's what I was thinking, Zoe!" Mom looked next at Joey, each of us taking our turn with her idea. "Joey, what do you think?" Baton tossed to the next in line.

Joey remained seated. She looked at me, then back at Mom. "Well, it kind of makes sense. Each of us has our own experience and skills. I've been a waitress forever and have done a lot of jobs at the Smokehouse Restaurant. I mean, it might work. Plus, I would love to be contributing more to a family legacy." The more Joey talked, the more she smiled and mirrored the gleam in Mom's eyes.

The focus shifted to me. Although I started this off, I pretty much got away with a non-answer. "Mom, you always come up with very creative ideas."

She clenched her jaw and narrowed her eyes. "I know. But what do you think? This could work, right?"

I wasn't getting off the hook with a neutral response. We were in too deep to escape this for another topic. The only way out was through it. "After my experience with working the books and managing the hotel, I feel like I could help out. But it would take all of us to make it successful." I left it there, with an obvious opening for the remaining sibling to speak. Frankly, it hinged on Harrison and his training as a chef to pull this off. I couldn't even believe we were having this conversation. I wondered how long this had been brewing in Mom's head. Probably decades.

Harrison sighed. I could tell by his hesitation that he didn't want to be the one dash Mom's dream. But realistically, what were the chances of him moving back and then all of us together running a restaurant? I shoved visions of our childhood out of my head. This was worlds away from that time. We had all grown and matured. And with less and less time left with Mom, maybe it was time to reunite as a family.

"I just don't know, Mom," Harrison said with the utmost kindness in his voice.

A tear formed in her eye. Her hands began to shake. She was watching her dream shatter before her eyes.

Before this devolved further, Harrison continued, "It would take a lot to make it happen."

"Oh, Harrison." Mom leapt up and in two steps grabbed him in a tight bear hug.

Over Mom's shoulder, Harrison's eyes widened at me. He pulled her back. "Mom, I didn't say yes." He locked eyes with her.

She nodded and sniffled. "But you didn't say no." She turned and looked at me. "If only we can solve the murder to ensure the hotel is safe."

"I'm working on it, Mom. I'm meeting the Emerald Hills PD later today." My confidence worked hard to make an appearance. It was possible we might never know how Ben was killed. That cloud hanging over the hotel might certainly permeate to another family business. I couldn't let that happen.

CHAPTER ELEVEN

My mind was completely consumed with the morning encounter at Mom's. Her desire for Harrison to move back to town consumed her. And now she might have created a path for that to happen. I stifled my excitement at the thought. So many things had to line up perfectly, and that seemed light years away. Front and center in my life was salvaging the hotel's reputation. We already had calls with several cancellations, and I feared the snowball had begun. I had to pour all of my energy into solving this mystery and repairing what I could.

I met Ty at the door of the lodge as he began unloading his lighting kits to set up for the event. He would get everything in place ahead of time and be ready for tomorrow evening's festivities.

"Hi Ty. Why don't you park everything here? Then you can set up wherever you like." I grabbed a couple of bags from him. I placed them in the corner, and he left to retrieve the remainder. I scooted everything around to make room and Ty returned with the final load.

The place hummed with the exact same activity from several days ago. I got a sense of déjà vu, minus Ben.

"Let me know what you need, Ty. I'll be inside for a while." I turned to leave and bumped into Marnee with her cat-eye glasses. She must have a color for every outfit. Today's were bright yellow. "That reminds me. Marnee, did you lose a pair of glasses? We found some that look just like those in another color, here in the lodge."

"Oh, thank you, Chloe. I wondered where those went." Marnee stepped toward Ty, dismissing me. "Ty, I'm thrilled to see your photography business doing so well."

Ty continued to carefully unpack and assemble the lighting kits. "Thank you, Mrs. Murano. I wouldn't be here without you." He stood. His cheeks drooped. "I'm so sorry about Ben. When I saw him fall, I hoped he would be OK." His voice quivered, reliving the trauma.

With my awkward presence, I extracted myself from the scene, just slow enough to overhear what was being said.

"Thank you, Ty. We're all still pretty shook up. But the show must go on, as they say," Marnee replied.

Ty tipped his head, appearing to try and interpret her peppy response.

"Keep up the good work, Ty. You've got amazing drive and talent. I'm just glad I could help make it happen in some small way. And you can call me Marnee. Mrs. Murano is my teacher persona."

Ty laughed. "That's just too weird. For now, I'll stick with Mrs. Murano."

"Well, if there's anything I can ever do for you, let me know." Marnee strutted across the room to the buffet tables being set up to supervise Carl and her team. As she passed the corner stage where the Sweet Adelines would perform, Marnee stuck her nose in the air. Janie stepped away from the podium, almost entering Marnee's path, and mimicked her response.

"Marnee, here's those glasses." I stepped between the two of them, averting a confrontation for now.

She snatched them out of my hand and stared Janie down.

"Marnee, why don't you walk me through the buffet setup?" I touched her elbow to turn her away from Janie. She jerked away from me and stomped toward the food tables. I followed, increasing the distance between the tension.

Marnee huffed. "That woman!" She pointed toward Janie. I hoped she didn't make me regret keeping them on as caterers. "I'm sorry to create a scene, Chloe. I know this is your event, and I'll tone it down." She turned toward the table and pointed to a dish with several pieces of skewered chicken. "This is what is replacing those dreadful meatballs. I think you'll love them." She handed me one to try.

I nibbled a bite and swallowed. Max suddenly appeared at my side and looked up at me with anticipation. I broke off a piece and fed it to him.

"I didn't make that for dog food," Marnee said. She snatched the stick with the remaining piece of chicken from my hand.

Max growled. Marnee took a step back, holding her free hand out as if to protect herself, misinterpreting his message. I understood loud and clear that it had nothing to do with the chicken and everything to do with Marnee's off-putting personality. Max did not like her.

I looked at him and he trotted off, pleased with a job well done.

Marnee waited until Max was on the other side of the room before continuing. "As I was saying, we've really elevated our food now that Carl is head chef. Frankly, I'm surprised Ben's food didn't kill someone before now. He had gotten so careless. Which I'm sure had everything to do with Janie." Marnee's voice had quieted. She appeared more hurt by Ben's affair than his death.

"Well, I'm glad you're here. I'm sure our guests will be thrilled with what you have prepared." Ty's head snapped up as he scanned the room for me. I held up an arm to indicate I'd be right there. "Holler if you need something."

I met Ty, who had his camera strapped around his neck. "I don't know if you had a chance to look at the pics I sent before for any feedback." He looked at me, seemingly unaware of what he had sent.

"Why don't we just start fresh? You take me around and show me your plan," I said.

"Cool." Surfer dude in full effect. He loped over to the performance stage and positioned his back to it. I tagged along. "I like to get the wide shots first, then get more close-ups later."

"OK," I replied. From what I saw in his sample photos, he clearly knew what he was doing and needed no input from me.

"I started here the other day when Ben was overseeing the food setup. Someone was handing out sample plates to everyone with those meatballs." He stopped, looked at me, and continued. "I can pretty much see the entire lodge from here. Then I go to the opposite corner and do the same thing so I can get the performance stage."

The lodge door opened and two uniformed Emerald Hills police officers entered. You could hear a pin drop. I needed to get this over with so we could move past this mystery.

"Ty, keep going. I trust your judgment." I continued to the front door and shook hands with the detectives. The whispers began. I led them to my office in the corner. At least we could start in private. I had bits and pieces to share, but nowhere near anything incriminating. I hoped to gain some comfort from their update that Ben's murder would soon be solved. From the corner of my eye, a buff-colored streak sprinted toward me. Max was not about to be left out of the briefing on the situation. The detectives looked doubtfully at Max. Little did they know. My pooch deserved a full-fledged badge, right alongside them.

CHAPTER TWELVE

Haley's eyes puffed with redness. She must not have gotten a wink of sleep since Ben's death. I reached over and grabbed her hand. "Haley, it will be OK. We'll get through this."

She nodded.

We were in the backroom of Caroline's Confections and Coffee Shop, confirming our dessert plans for the grand re-opening. Caroline had piled a plate high with gingersnaps for Max while she, Haley and I planned the menu. The quiet was a welcome respite from the hectic several days since this ordeal began.

"Why don't you give Max a treat?" I asked. He dutifully sat between Caroline and me, waiting for his first course. She had thoroughly trained him to expect something every time he came in. She even made gingerbread cookies in the shape of a dog. He wasn't spoiled at all.

Haley took a treat from the pile and held her arm out. Max came to Haley's side of the table and looked at her, total compassion in his eyes, before he gobbled the cookie. Haley smiled. My boy could brighten anyone's day. She looked at me and I nodded. She fed him round two. Not so mannerly this time, he munched loudly. We laughed. It felt good to release that tension.

I turned in my chair and faced my notepad. "I hope you've got plenty of supplies for those gingersnaps. I think we may need to double the order. And since we're expecting a bit more snow, I think we should double the hot chocolate supplies as well. I have a feeling that sleigh ride is going to get a lot of action."

Caroline grabbed a gingersnap and took a bite. Max whimpered. "There's plenty to share, my friend." She took another bite and handed the rest to Max. More demurely this time, he ate the remainder. "It seems like the dessert menu is set. Is Murano's still able to cater?" Caroline looked to Haley to see her reaction.

"I'm OK, Aunt Caroline. It was just such a shock," Haley said.

"Actually, Marnee seems like she hasn't missed a beat. She did change the menu. Apparently she has swapped those meatballs that were Ben's specialty for chicken sates. She and Carl really complained about those meatballs when I was there a few days ago. I don't get it. But the chicken was very good too. So I'll leave the menu to the experts."

Haley sniffled. She was putting on a brave face. Max placed his snout on her thigh. She laid her hand on his head. "I know Ben was kind of mean. But I liked him. When he taught classes at culinary school, I think he was just hard on us so we would get better."

I looked at Caroline and back at Haley. "I didn't know Ben taught there."

Haley nodded. "Marnee did too. They were always fighting before and after class. Marnee tried to be the main person teaching. I actually think she was better than Ben and he didn't like that."

"Hmmm." I made a note on a different page in my notebook. That might explain Marnee's apparent euphoria and confidence in managing the restaurant. She was angling for the limelight all along.

"Chloe." Caroline turned in her chair. "What's going on?"

I looked at both of them. "I don't really want to say until I know anything for sure. The police detectives were out at the hotel yesterday. And you know how fast rumors travel."

Caroline nodded, being the subject of one of those devastating stories not that long ago. "Are they close to solving?" Caroline peeked at Haley, not yet revealing what we knew about her candy.

Haley fidgeted in her seat. "Haley," Caroline said. "What's going on?"

"Well, I don't know," she replied quietly enough that Caroline and I both leaned forward to hear. She kept her head down.

Caroline reached over and grabbed Haley's hand. "Hon." That was all it took for the waterworks to begin. Caroline left the room and returned with a box of tissues.

Haley grabbed some with both hands. Max half-climbed into Haley's lap, giving her a hug. That broke the tension. She chuckled and hugged back. With her head still down, she whispered, "I don't want to spread rumors, but Ty told me that Marnee thought Ben was cheating." She paused, looked up, and returned her gaze to her lap, fidgeting with the tissues. "Marnee hired Ty to spy on Ben and take pictures for her. I didn't think it was right and didn't want him to do it. I guess she paid him a lot of money for it."

I looked at Caroline and nodded. "I'm sorry you got wrapped up in that, Haley," I said.

She sat taller in her chair. "I asked Ty not to do it. I mean, Ben was no angel. And Marnee didn't deserve what he was doing to her. I just didn't want Ty mixed up in that mess. He's such a nice kid. And he's been through so much."

"This had nothing to do with you or Ty, Haley," Caroline interjected. "Those two made their own mess."

My eyes widened. Was Caroline going to spill the beans on the suspicion about Haley's candy? I hoped not. Now was not the time, if ever. I wished with my whole being that answers about Ben's death would clearly appear so we could officially cross Haley and her candy off the list of suspects.

"I know," Haley answered, oblivious to the insinuation, thankfully. "It's just that Marnee was so pushy with Ty. I don't think he really wanted to get involved either. I mean, he's so relaxed, but the stress of following Ben around really upset him." Haley straightened fully in her seat and pushed up her sleeves, as if ready for baking marathon. "Sometimes, adults are the worst. If you have a problem with someone, just tell them to their face."

Caroline read Haley like a book. She reached her hand over to me, signaling patience while we waited for Haley to continue.

Right on cue, Haley grabbed a gingersnap, got up from her chair, and started pacing. That poor girl's nerves looked frayed. Max trailed right behind her, licking up crumbs as they were dropped.

"Haley," Caroline prompted.

She stopped and returned to her seat, grabbing another wad of tissues. "Aunt Caroline, it just wasn't right. I should have stayed out of it. But Ty was so upset having to do this for Marnee. I hated to see my friend that way. I just wanted this to be over."

Haley collapsed her head and arms onto the table, inconsolable. Caroline sped over, hugged her, and rubbed her back. Max looked at me and jumped into the chair next to Haley, joining in the comfort. This drama got more complicated by the hour.

CHAPTER THIRTEEN

The powdery snowfall greeted us as we approached Lily Lodge, the crown jewel in our new treehouse hotel complex. The lights shone from inside, ready for a celebration. The atmosphere was much more festive than I felt. A knot grew in my stomach. The culprit for Ben's murder was still at large. Max and I trudged up the steps and inside, where we would oversee the final preparations. Through the door, the warmth was promising. My gut told me that Max and I were closing in on the clues, with just one key piece left to be revealed. Looking at my watch, I knew the countdown was on to the event kick-off. Maybe one last foray through the lodge to see what we may have missed.

Cinnamon permeated the air with our hot-spiced cider ready to be served up. Evergreen boughs adorned the staircases. And the damaged railing from where Ben had toppled looked like new. There was no sign that a tragedy had ever occurred. The twinkling strands of lights draped from corner to corner. The performance stage, the food tables, the photo booth. It was all coming together. And to top it all off, a roaring fire. If not for the pall of the mystery, this would be perfect. I pulled my chin up. I needed to put on a good face.

Haley looked like she had bounced back from the emotion of our meeting the other day. She had a smile on her face, relaxed shoulders, and a bounce in her step. I approached the dessert table, which she had prepared to look like a work of art. She had outdone herself, not only with the delectable sweets, but the presentation of them in a way that made you feel guilty for disturbing the design.

"Hi, Haley." Max stood dutifully at my side, ready for any and all requests.

Her head bobbed up. "Hi, Chloe!" she practically yelled. "What do you think?" She waved her arm along the dessert table, a gleam in her eye. She reached over and picked up a little piece of a cookie. "And I didn't forget you." She bent to feed Max a gingersnap.

He smiled wide and scooted closer to her for seconds.

"Haley, this is magnificent." I hugged her. "I can't tell you how grateful I am that you're here. My guests will be so happy. I'm just sorry we have to disturb your gorgeous creations."

She tipped her head back and laughed, more relaxed than I'd seen her in a while. As she was about to give Max another cookie, he sped to the door. Trixie and Mom had arrived. My personable boy, always the greeter.

I carefully extracted one of Haley's mini chocolate tarts from the stand so that no one noticed it was missing. I popped it into my mouth and closed my eyes.

"She does good work, doesn't she?"

I jumped and turned to see Carl had sidled next to me. I nodded while wiping crumbs from my mouth. I finished the tart and said, "Yes, she does. This might just be the most popular stop of the night."

Carl moved around me and took a candy from the table. "These are my favorite. When she had those raspberry-filled ones the other day, I think I ate half of them." He tossed the candy in the air into his mouth and chewed with his mouth open, smacking his lips. Thankfully, his attire was presentable with his chef jacket buttoned and clean pants that fit.

My head swiveled toward him. "You ate some of the candy the other day?" I took a step back.

"Lots of people did." He grabbed another candy and inhaled it.

"Carl!" Haley admonished. "Save some for the guests."

He held a hand up. "Sorry, they're just so addicting."

If other people in addition to Ben ate the candy, then it couldn't have possibly been the poison that killed him. That let Haley off the hook, but now who was the most likely culprit?

Carl had a small bit of drool escaping the side of his mouth. "Maybe I can talk to Marnee and see if you could make some of the desserts for Murano's."

Haley clasped her hands under her chin. That girl was going places with her talent. "That would be amazing." She giggled. "I'm just sorry I didn't get to taste the famous meatballs the other day. Maybe I can try them at the restaurant."

Carl shook his head. "Nah, they're long gone. But, really, you didn't miss anything. They were overhyped."

Haley's eyebrows furrowed. She looked at me, then back to Carl. "Huh. That's weird. Ben said they were the best he ever had the other day when you gave him the samples."

Carl grabbed two more candies and stuck them in his pocket. He leaned forward and whispered, "Actually, it was Marnee's recipe. Everyone thought Ben had created it. Even so, we had to modernize the Murano's menu. Ever since we did that, it's been standing room only." Carl turned and practically skipped away.

Something was off about that guy. I just couldn't place it. My phone buzzed. I expected it to be quite a bit busier during the setup. But given that we had already done this once, everyone knew what they needed to do. The notification said I had an e-mail from Marnee. That was strange, since she was supposed to be here with the setup. I opened the mail to see a cryptic message. Something about your sister Janie and now we can live our dream. It certainly wasn't meant for me. But who was the intended recipient?

With my nose buried in my phone, I didn't see Paul come up to me.

"Chloe, this is all coming together so beautifully. You've done an amazing job." He smiled warmly.

I shook my head. "Sorry, what did you say?"

"Is everything OK?" He gestured toward my phone.

"Oh, yeah. It's nothing. I just need to make a phone call. Say, can you do me a favor? I've lost track of Max. Would you please corral him and make sure he's not pestering the reindeer? A stampede is the last thing I need on my hands."

He laughed and turned to leave. "Sure thing. And maybe when you get a break, you and I can take a sleigh ride." His eyes pleaded.

I zombie-walked to my office, Paul's request a faint presence, the sounds of celebration muffled by my thoughts of another dramatic incident. Why hadn't I seen it sooner? It was right in front of me. I was losing a step in solving these mysteries. The stress of the last year weighed heavily on me. Moving back to Cedarbrook. Mending my relationship with Mom. And more than a full-time job with the hotel management and expansion. Maybe I needed more of a break than I realized. I steeled myself for the call. After that, I had to suit up with my game face and make this event the talk of the town for years to come. My gift to Mom.

CHAPTER FOURTEEN

R elief enveloped me as I exited the office. I finally had answers to those questions that had plagued me for days. The festivities were in full swing. The top of the hour approached when I would kick off the official grand re-opening of the hotel. Nobody was the wiser of what was about to happen. That was probably a good thing. Harrison and his family had arrived. He looked in deep conversation with Pearl, catching up on old times. The kids were enjoying the photo booth with props and goofy faces. Mom was dressed in a gorgeous red number with low-slung heels. Joey had done Mom's hair up in a beautiful chignon bun. I needed to run down Ty and ask him to get a family portrait before the evening ended. This would be a night for the history books. Everything had finally come together just as we had planned.

I stepped farther into the growing, bustling crowd. Joey and Zoey entered the lodge, arm in arm. The hotel expansion had turned out to be a pivotal event in bringing our family back together. I longed for this to be the start of a new era for the Carsons. I worked my way around the room, greeting all of the guests. The food was a big hit, and Haley's dessert table had been decimated. She looked so relaxed as she hurriedly served each customer. We made eye contact, and I gave her a small clap of my hands.

The Sweet Adelines belted out "Winter Wonderland" as a few people hit the dance floor. I continued my stroll around the lower level. I spotted several gnomes that I had permitted Mom to bring inside to the lodge. Those things multiplied like rabbits. I was doubtful people would take to them, but they had become a huge hit at the hotel. The song ended, and the singers were taking a short break before the opening act in a few minutes. Janie stepped down from the podium and approached Carl. They embraced, serious expressions on their faces. What I wouldn't give to hear that conversation.

The door to the lodge opened and released a cold rush of air inside. Buzz led the way ahead of two uniformed officers. All heads swiveled toward the distraction. Murmurs began. I swallowed and stepped forward. Buzz looked at me and I pointed toward Carl. The entourage continued toward the buffet table and announced Carl was under arrest for the murder of Ben Murano. Carl stood defiantly still. The officers forced his arms behind him and fastened the handcuffs while reading him his rights.

Janie fell to her knees and screamed, "You can't do that!" She buried her head in her hands. The rest of her quartet surrounded her, the sequined gowns shimmering bright. Her cries echoed off the expansive ceiling. She struggled to stand and pointed at Carl. "He only did it for me."

The officers led Carl from the lodge as the whispers grew louder. "Chloe, what's happening?" I turned to see Marnee with tears in her eyes and her hand over her heart. "This can't be true. Carl swore to me he had nothing to do with it." Marnee collapsed into a chair. I bent over and firmly embraced her. That woman had been through the ringer.

"I'm so sorry, Marnee. I think Carl fooled a lot of us, including Ben." I knelt next to her.

She lifted her chin, her eyes and nose dripping. "How?" was all she could say.

I shook my head. "Ironically, it was the meatballs."

She tipped her head. "It was the meatballs?"

I nodded. "Carl poisoned them, and Ben ate them the day of the dress rehearsal. The fall over the railing only happened because he had collapsed."

Marnee buried her head in her arms. In the distance I heard the faint sounds of a piano being played. I stood and scanned the room. In the corner, Harrison had begun playing a soothing tune. I had no idea he knew how to play. He continued, increasing the volume. The effect of the music broke the tension. I approached the microphone, not exactly sure how I follow all of that, willing the words to emerge by the time I got there.

I cleared my throat, looked at Harrison, and waited for him to pause. "Ladies and gentleman." I looked around. "From the bottom of my heart, thank you." I paused. "Thank you for coming to support us with the grand re-opening. I'm very sorry our celebration was interrupted, but I'm pleased that Carl will see justice for what he did to Ben." I panned the crowd. I think people were torn between applauding and crying. I looked at Harrison. He quietly began to play again, a song with an upbeat tone. "Please continue enjoying yourselves as best you can." I stepped down from the podium, hoping we could salvage the evening.

Mom stepped away from the crowd and headed to the piano. She hugged Harrison, and the two of them exchanged a look of love. That right there was worth all of the drama. Something I never thought I would see. Their relationship on the mend. Mom headed my direction with the most relaxed look I had seen on her in quite some time. "Chloe, you've outdone yourself. This is a magnificent start to the next phase of our lives." Mission accomplished.

My eyes darted around, and I realized I hadn't seen Max in quite some time. With the distraction of the arrest, I had forgotten Paul was on the hunt to find him. My heart beat faster. What would I do if my faithful companion was lost? I couldn't take it. I looked toward the door as it opened with Paul coming through. Max darted past his legs, snow clinging to his paws. I bent down to receive my sprinting pal. I took him in and closed my eyes. When I opened them, Paul was right next to me with a box, holding something that was making small peeps. He tipped it down to show me Trixie and four of the most darling little puppies I had ever seen. Mom sped over and poked her head in the box. Max was jumping and yelping. Paul set the box down and Max stuck his head inside, sniffing every tiny little body.

I held my hands up. "Could this night get any more exciting?"

Paul laughed. "Max led me to them. Apparently Trixie had wandered off to have the puppies."

I looked at Mom and laughed. "You were right after all. Trixie wasn't fat, she was pregnant."

She had a blank look on her face. "Are you sure?"

I leaned my head back and pointed to the box. "The evidence is right there."

"Chloe, what am I going to do with five dogs?" She staggered to the fireplace hearth and sat with a dazed look that mirrored how we all felt.

"We'll figure it out, Mom." I sat next to her and grabbed her hand. "Why don't you take them to the office for now?" I pointed. Paul and our town veterinarian followed my directions with Max in tow. This night was one for the books. Our quiet little Cedarbrook had exploded tonight with enough commotion to last us another decade. Harrison continued to entertain us with his musical talent.

Paul exited the office with Max prancing by his side. He sat to my right on the hearth, reaching for my hand. He looked me in the eye and asked, "Chloe, would you like to go on a sleigh ride with me?" A squeal came from my left. I slowly blinked and smiled. "Yes." A second squeal escaped from my left. Max jumped onto my lap. "I think that's a yes from both of us." I put Max on the floor and stood. Paul and I left the lodge, hand-in-hand, with a cocker spaniel strutting right alongside.

CHAPTER FIFTEEN

The banquet room at Lily Lodge remained decorated after the completion of the grand re-opening event. It was the only place in town large enough to host our family dinner. This get together left a gleam in Mom's eye that I expected to last for months. I would have bet a lot of money it never would have happened, for a myriad of reasons. Mom's determination and steadfast focus on reuniting her family never wavered. That woman had been a rock to all of her kids for decades. Coming together in harmony was the least we could do for her. She sat at the head of the table, the matriarch in charge, and Harrison sat at the opposite end. There were almost twenty of us Carsons around the oblong table.

I had talked Caroline into helping with the meal so that I could enjoy my family time. The Smokehouse Restaurant catered our dinner and rivaled the quality of food provided by the Murano Grill. But I'm getting ahead of myself. We even had the extended family of pups in attendance. Mama Trixie was completely in charge of those growing little furballs. And Max did his best to help corral them.

I looked around the table, soaking up the atmosphere. The weary faces belied the raucous atmosphere. The exhaustion of the last few days was set aside for this historic occasion. Who knew when this might ever happen again?

Mom was unusually quiet but rose with her glass of wine in hand. She tapped it with a spoon to garner attention. The room quieted, all eyes on Mabel. Her gaze circled every single person at the table, imprinting their faces in her memory. Her voice cracked as she began to speak. "I can't tell you how happy I am at this very moment." She paused, savoring every second of the limelight. "My vision of a family reunion never wavered, right Chloe?" She gestured toward me.

I shrugged. "You know how determined our mom is," I said. Everyone laughed, knowing that was code for *she's very stubborn when she sets her mind on something.*

Mom continued, raising her glass, "Here's to many more family dinners. And bigger and better things for the hotel. Cheers!"

We all raised our glass and in unison sang "Cheers!"

Our bookings since Ben's murder had significantly slowed. But once word got out that Carl had been arrested, the phone rang off the hook. Our little out-of-the-way treehouses had become a destination for some very large conferences and retreats.

Mom took her seat but continued in the spotlight. "Chloe." All heads turned toward me. We all knew it was coming. Mom led the way for this room filled with matchmakers.

My face heated up. I kept my eyes forward and sipped a drink of ice water.

"We know that you and Paul went on a sleigh ride. Spill the beans," Mom ordered. The group started chanting *spill the beans.*

I knew exactly what they wanted. But if I said it out loud, I might never hear the end of it. Truthfully, either way, my family would relentlessly pester me. I held up a hand to silence the unruly bunch. You could hear a pin drop. "OK. Paul asked me out. And I said yes."

The cheer that rose from the crowd resembled a small football stadium after the home team scored. "Where are you going?" someone yelled.

I shook my head. "No more."

Mom stood again, ready to toast again. "Maybe next year, we'll be having a wedding at the lodge," she said.

Max bolted from his sentry post in the corner and stood next to me, eyes pleading. "You too, Max?" He jumped on my lap and licked my cheek.

Mom continued. She was on a roll. "The last piece to the puzzle is our family restaurant. What do you think Harrison?" Mom sat and looked directly ahead at him at the other end of the table, almost challenging him to say no.

He smiled. "I guess judging by the fact we came for a visit, I'll offer an answer of never say never." I was certain Mom wouldn't settle for that answer. Even for Harrison to consider it was tremendous progress and might just tide Mom over for now.

Marnee had closed the Murano Grill and put it up for sale. Their business was going gangbusters, but I think the memory was too much for her. With her passion for cooking, she decided to move to France and attend the Le Cordon Bleu culinary school. With the Murano's building already set up as a restaurant, we would essentially just have to move in. But it was a long way from a done deal. Our little town needed some time and space to heal from the recent events.

Carl's selfishness had ruined many lives. His anger at Ben's treatment of his sister Janie had blinded him. Ben had broken many promises to Janie of a life of luxury.

Haley and Ty didn't seem much worse for the wear. Youth can compensate for a lot of trials. With Ty's talent, he'd been contacted by a movie producer to intern the next year. And Haley's future at Caroline's was all but secured after her debut during our celebration. Yes, all had righted itself with our world, for now.

Hear From Max

Max tells his side of the story. Scan the QR code below with your device's camera to find out the scoop straight from the pooch's mouth.

NEXT RELEASE - CROCUSES AND CORPSES

C hloe and Max are looking forward to a relaxing cruise before the treehouse hotel busy season begins. But after a trip to the ship's hair salon with her mom, Chloe quickly finds herself mired in a mysterious murder.

Luke's sweet-talkin' of the ladies, and his one-of-a-kind hair styles earned him huge tips and the adoration of his clients. But Chloe and Max quickly discover that Luke's carefully coiffed hair and charming chatter were a facade for lies that ran deep.

As Chloe and Max navigate the festive, fun-loving cruise, they un cover deceit, jealousy and diabolical schemes that threaten the hotel and her mom's future. Can they crack the clues to Luke's demise be- fore the murderer sinks their vacation plans in *Crocuses and Corpses*?

Scan the QR code below with your device's camera to order now.

Thank You

Thank you for reading **Mistletoe and Misfortune.** Reviews are crucial for helping other readers discover new books.. If you want to share your love for this book, please leave a review for other readers. I'd really appreciate it!

Scan the QR code below with your device's camera to leave a review.

About the Author

Sue Hollowell is a wife and empty nester with a lot of mom left over. Not far from her everyday thoughts are dreams of visiting tropical locations. She likes cake and the more frosting the better!

Scan the QR code below with your device's camera to follow her author page on Facebook.